This book belongs to

★ Lily   From Aunt DO and Uncle Mark ★

Sandy Creek
NEW YORK

An Imprint of Sterling Published
387 Park Avenue South
New York, NY 10016

ISBN 978-1-4351-3752-3

Manufactured in Guangzhou, China
Lot #:
10 9 8 7 6 5
8/12

The Magical Ballet Slippers

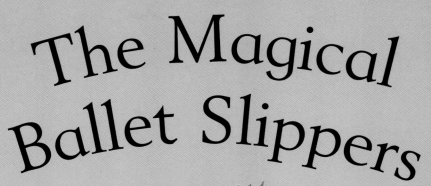

Written by Nick Ellsworth ★ Illustrated by Veronica Vasylenko

Sandy Creek

Lily, a ballerina, was hurrying to the theater. Today was the day of the Grand Ballet. Lily was dancing with her friends Wanda, Amber, and Tilly. They were all looking forward to dancing with Fleur.

Fleur was the prima ballerina, and everyone loved her, especially Lily.

"Fleur is such a wonderful dancer," sighed Lily. "I wish that I could dance like her one day."

Fleur always danced in a magical pair of silver ballet slippers. Only the prima ballerina could wear them. They would not work properly if anyone else wore them.

They all loved to dance with
Fleur, and watched her closely
as she performed a perfect plié,

a beautiful arabesque,

and a stunning pirouette.

As the first dance ended, everyone clapped as the
dancers followed Fleur offstage. They hurried to
change their costumes for the next dance.

Suddenly, Fleur appeared in her bare feet, looking very upset.
"Something terrible has happened!" Fleur exclaimed. "I took off my
silver ballet slippers to retie them, and now they have disappeared.
I won't be able to dance again until they are found."

"You mustn't worry," said Lily kindly. "We'll get them back for you."

"I'll look in the woods," said Wanda, hurrying out of the door.

"I'll look in the meadow," said Amber, as she ran off quickly.

"I'll look in the yard," said Tilly, dashing after her friends.

"We'll find the slippers in time for the next dance," Lily promised.

As Lily wondered which way she should go, she spotted a raven flying toward the woods. She could see something silver dangling from its beak.

"The silver slippers!" gasped Lily. "I'll have to run fast to keep up with that raven." And she ran after it.

Meanwhile, the ballet
slippers grew too heavy
for the raven.
They fell from its beak.
        The slippers
dropped right in front of
Wanda, who was searching
the woods.

   "The magical slippers!"
she said. "How beautiful
they are. I'll just try them
on quickly."

But, as soon as Wanda put on the
magic slippers, a strange thing
happened. She danced a plié.
She danced pliés up and down
and up and down, until she
realized she couldn't stop.
"Help me someone!" she cried, as
she danced faster and faster.
Not far away, Lily could see
her friend bobbing up and down
in the distance.
"I hope Wanda's all right," she
thought, hurrying toward her.
But poor Wanda pliéd out of the
woods and into the meadow.

Wanda's legs were so tired she couldn't dance anymore,
and she fell flat on her back into a nearby bush.
"Are you all right?" asked Amber, who had been searching the meadow.
"Yes, thanks," puffed Wanda. "But please help me take these slippers off."
Amber pulled off the magical ballet slippers and gazed at them.
"They're so beautiful," she said. "I'm sure no one would mind if I tried
them on quickly." Not far off, Lily was rushing through the woods,
trying to catch up as fast as she could.

Amber tried on the magical slippers and
she danced a perfect arabesque.
"I never knew I could arabesque so well!" she thought. Then she
did another, and another, until she realized that she couldn't stop.
"Help! I can't stop!" poor Amber called, as she danced out of the
meadow and into the yard.

By this time, Lily had caught up with Wanda
and helped her out of the bush.
"Where are Fleur's ballet slippers?" she asked.
"Amber tried them on, and now she can't
stop dancing," puffed Wanda.
"Quick, we must follow her," cried Lily rushing off.

Amber was so dizzy from dancing that she ended up
in the fountain with a large splash.
"Help me out of here, someone!" she shouted, splashing around. Luckily,
Tilly was nearby and ran to help. But when she saw the silver slippers
lying on the ground, she just couldn't resist putting them on.
"They're so beautiful," she said. "I'm sure no one would mind
if I tried them on quickly."

But when Tilly tried on the magical
slippers, a strange thing happened.
She started to pirouette around
and around.

"Wheee ... this is fun!" exclaimed Tilly.
"I never knew I could pirouette so well!"

But then she began to spin faster and faster
and realized that she couldn't stop.

Lily and Wanda reached the fountain and helped Amber out of the water. "Where are Fleur's ballet slippers?" asked Lily. "Tilly put them on and now she can't stop dancing," replied Amber. "We'd better follow her," said Lily.

Poor Tilly danced a pirouette down the hill and straight into a muddy puddle.

The others caught up with her and helped her up.

Lily carefully took the precious ballet slippers off Tilly's feet.

"They are so beautiful," said Lily, and she wanted to try them on too. But in her heart, she knew that there was only one person who was meant to wear them.

"Let's return the slippers to the prima ballerina," she said to the others. "She'll be so happy we found them."

"My slippers!" exclaimed Fleur when
Lily and the others returned.
"How can I ever thank you?"
Fleur gave Lily a silver charm in the
shape of her silver ballet slippers.

It looked just like them.
"Thank you!" said Lily gratefully.
"I'll treasure it forever!"

"Now, we must finish the show," said Fleur, looking around at the girls. But Wanda, Amber, and Tilly were in such a mess they couldn't go back onstage.

"Oh, dear!" Fleur sighed. "You won't be able to dance looking like that." Then Fleur turned to Lily with a smile. "We will dance together."

Back at the Grand Ballet, Lily danced with the prima ballerina. They danced a plié, an arabesque, and a pirouette. And they danced so beautifully together that everyone clapped and cheered more than ever before.

The magical silver charm helped Lily to dance the most beautiful dance of her life.

"I'll remember this evening for ever and ever," thought Lily, as she walked to the front of the stage, and took her final bow.